A Tooth Is Loose

Written by Lisa Trumbauer
Illustrated by Steve Gray

Children's Press®
A Division of Scholastic Inc.
New York • Toronto • London • Auckland • Sydney
Mexico City • New Delhi • Hong Kong
Danbury, Connecticut

**For my parents, Fred and Sigrid Trutkoff, the catchers
of all loose teeth**
—L.T.

To Pammy Gray for her brave trip to Dr. Nagy's dentist chair
—S.G.

Reading Consultants

Linda Cornwell
Literacy Specialist

Katharine A. Kane
Education Consultant
(Retired, San Diego County Office of Education
and San Diego State University)

Library of Congress Cataloging-in-Publication Data

Trumbauer, Lisa, 1963-
   A tooth is loose / written by Lisa Trumbauer ; illustrated by Steve Gray.
      p. cm. – (A rookie reader)
   Summary: Illustrations and rhyming text describe how loose teeth come out.
   ISBN 0-516-23445-5 (lib. bdg.)   0-516-25841-9 (pbk.)
   [1. Teeth–Fiction. 2. Stories in rhyme.] I. Gray, Steve, 1950- ill.
II. Title. III. Series.
   PZ8.3.T753To 2004
   [E]–dc22
                                              2003016584

CHILDREN'S PRESS, and A ROOKIE READER®, and associated logos are trademarks and or
registered trademarks of Scholastic Library Publishing. SCHOLASTIC and associated logos are
trademarks and or registered trademarks of Scholastic Inc.
1 2 3 4 5 6 7 8 9 10 R 13 12 11 10 09 08 07 06 05 04

A tooth is loose!

We lose our baby teeth.

A tooth is loose!

It is sometimes hard to eat.

A tooth is loose!
You can make it wiggle.

A tooth is loose!
You can make it jiggle.

Wiggle it with your finger.
Wiggle it with your tongue.

You can feel it wiggle.
Wiggling is fun.

You can wiggle in the park.
You can wiggle in the pool.

I hope it does not wiggle out
when you are at school.

19

A tooth is loose!
You must treat it with care.

The tooth is out!
A new one will grow there.

Word List (47 words)

a	hard	not	tongue
are	hope	one	tooth
at	I	our	treat
baby	in	out	we
can	is	park	when
care	it	pool	wiggle
does	jiggle	school	wiggling
eat	loose	sometimes	will
feel	lose	teeth	with
finger	make	the	you
fun	must	there	your
grow	new	to	

About the Author

Lisa Trumbauer remembers losing her last tooth when she bit into a grilled cheese sandwich. The author of nearly 200 books for children, both fiction and nonfiction, Lisa still likes to eat grilled cheese sandwiches. She lives in New Jersey with her dog, two cats, and her husband Dave, who, Lisa claims, makes the best grilled cheese sandwiches on the planet.

About the Illustrator

When Steve Gray isn't busy drawing and painting, he likes to golf and play drums with his band "Flying Utensils."